ARCHITECTURE

EVERY LINE HAS A STORY

PURVA SINGH RATHORE

ISBN: 978-93-340-6509-1

DEDICATION

This book is dedicated to the calling to write a story on architecture differently. The art to see beyond the walls, line, buildings and spaces that whispers a story of adventure within. May it inspire others to see architecture from different point of views.

CONTENTS

ACKNOWLEDGMENTS

I would like to express my heartfelt gratitude to everyone who encouraged me to bring this dream filled journey to life. This book was born from love for architecture and the stories of adventure hidden in spaces, lines, floor-plans. The strength to transform imagination into words for the readers that keep inspiring the architecture was magical. I'm deeply grateful, for the journey that inspires me to write.

A DREAM CITY

When I was a child, I thought buildings were just walls and windows. It wasn't until I became an architect that I realized every line drawn has a purpose, a meaning, a story to tell. Every wall, every curve, every blueprint carries the dreams of those who built it and the stories of those who live within it. They say every line drawn by an architect tells a story. But what if some lines whisper secrets from the past?

So...... It all started with a childhood sketch.

I remember sitting at my small wooden desk, a box of colored pencils spread out before me. I was no more than ten years old, lost in a world of imagination. My tiny hands moved across the paper, sketching an entire city tall towers, bridges, winding streets, a grand plaza at the heart of it all. It was a city unlike anything I had ever seen before. I filled every corner with details, elegant archways, mysterious alleys, hidden courtyards.

I called it *My Dream City*.

I didn't just draw buildings, I created stories for them. There was a grand library that held books from forgotten times, a café where people shared their deepest secrets, a towering mansion that no one dared to enter. It was a city filled with mystery and wonder, a place that only existed in my mind.

Or so I thought.

Years passed, and I pursued my passion for architecture. I studied, learned, and designed real buildings. My childhood sketches faded into the background, forgotten in old notebooks and dusty drawers. Until one day, everything changed.

I had been invited to a project overseas, a dream opportunity to work on a large-scale urban development. The location? A small, lesser-known town across the ocean, a place I had never been before. As I stepped off the plane and drove through the city, a strange feeling settled in my chest. The streets, the plazas, the buildings—it all felt eerily familiar.

And then I saw it.

A fountain in the center of the main square, surrounded by cobbled pathways and archways that led into a bustling marketplace. My heart pounded. It was identical to the one I had drawn as a child. I stood frozen, staring in disbelief. How could this be? How could a place I had imagined sketched in a small notebook decades ago exist in reality?

I tried to shake it off as a coincidence. Maybe I had seen pictures of this place somewhere before. Maybe my childhood imagination wasn't as original as I thought. But the deeper I explored, the more unsettling it became. There was the library with its grand wooden doors. The cafe on the corner where people whispered secrets over coffee. Even the mansion at the end of the road the one I had drawn with locked gates and looming towers stood exactly as I had envisioned it. But something was wrong. Determined to find answers, I started asking around. The locals spoke of old legends, of an unknown architect who had designed the city many years ago. But no one knew his name, and no records of his work existed.

Then, I found something that sent shivers down my spine.

An old bookstore at the edge of town held a collection of dusty architectural drawings. As I flipped through them, my breath caught in my throat. The lines, the structures, the designs they were mine. My childhood sketches, aged and yellowed as if they had been drawn long before I was even born.

How was this possible?

Desperate for answers, I searched for the oldest resident of the town, an old man who had lived there for nearly a century. When I showed him the sketches, his eyes widened in shock.

“This city,” he whispered, “was designed by a young architect long ago. But he vanished before it was ever built.”

I felt a chill run down my spine. *Vanished?*

He led me to an abandoned house on the outskirts of town. Dust covered all surface, and old blueprints were scattered across a wooden desk. I picked one up and gasped.

It was my drawing. My childhood sketches. But it had been redrawn in a hand that was not mine, signed with initials I didn't recognize.

And then, I saw the portrait.

A faded black-and-white photograph of a man young, with piercing eyes. He looked a little familiar. My hands shook as I stared at the image, my mind struggling to make sense of it. The old man placed a trembling hand on my shoulder. "They say he disappeared one night, leaving behind only his designs. Some believe he was never meant to exist in this time."

I couldn't breathe. Was it possible? Could it be that I had designed this city... in another life?

Suddenly, memories flooded my mind—flashes of another time, another era. The feel of ink on my fingers, the weight of a drafting pencil, the sound of construction echoing in the distance. I saw myself, not as I was now, but as *him*, standing where I stood, designing the city I had always dreamed of.

A wave of dizziness hit me, and I stumbled back. The walls around me seemed to close in, whispers filling the air, as if the lines I had drawn were speaking back to me.

I had built this city. Not in this life, but in another.

And now, I had returned.

The realization sent a shiver down my spine. My childhood sketch had been more than just imagination. It had been a memory—a blueprint of a past I had long forgotten, but one that had found a way to come alive once more.

As I walked through the streets again, everything looked different. The city wasn't just a place it was a story. A story I had written long ago, in another lifetime. And now, I was here again, walking through the lines of my own creation, unraveling a mystery that had been waiting for me to return.

Maybe architecture was more than just buildings. Maybe every line really did have a story. And maybe, just maybe, some stories were meant to be told across lifetimes.

THE SKETCH FROM ONATHER LIFE

Every cobbled street, every archway, every tower standing against the sky I knew them, not just because I had drawn them, but because I had lived them. The air carried a strange familiarity, as though the past had never truly left. And now, I was beginning to remember. The more I walked through the streets, the more the visions came. They weren't just fleeting images anymore. They were memories, as vivid as the present, pulling me back into a time before this life.

I was no longer just me I was him.

A young architect in an era long gone. I could feel the weight of my drafting tools in my hand, the rough texture of parchment beneath my fingers. The flickering light of oil lamps illuminated my desk as I sketched the lines that would one day become this city.

But the dream city was never meant to be built so easily.

I saw myself fighting for my vision, struggling against forces determined to bury my designs. The city's rulers powerful, greedy, resistant to change mocked my ambition. *"Your designs are too bold, too different. Stick to what is safe,"* they had said. But I had refused to conform. This city wasn't just a plan on paper. It was a masterpiece waiting to come alive.

Then came the sabotage.

Blueprints stolen in the dead of night. Designs mysteriously altered. Materials arriving warped and unusable. It was as if someone re or something was trying to stop me. And then, the worst blow of all: my patron, the one noble who had believed in my vision, suddenly disappeared without a trace. His support had been my only shield against the corruption that threatened to swallow my project whole.

I was left alone. No funds, no backing, only my relentless dream.

And then... the fire.

I gasped, stumbling back into the present. My hands trembled as the visions faded, leaving only the lingering scent of smoke in my mind. The mansion at the end of the road—the one I had drawn locked and abandoned—was more than just a mystery.

It was my home.

Or rather, *his* home. My home, in another life.

I had lived there, breathed in the very air that now filled its decaying halls. And it was there that the fire had started, consuming my blueprints, my work, my dreams. The flames had erased me from history. But how? Had it been an accident? Or something darker?

I had to know.

The answers lay inside that mansion. And this time, I wouldn't run from the past I would face it.

I turned towards the house, its looming silhouette standing against the darkening sky. The lines of my past had led me here.

And now, they would reveal the truth.

The memories came in fragments at first shadows of another time, blurred images, whispers of conversations I had never heard before. But the longer I stayed in this city, the clearer they became. I wasn't just remembering the past; I was reliving it.

That night, I stood before the grand mansion—the same one from my childhood sketch. Its towering presence loomed over me, its iron gates rusted yet firm, as if guarding the secrets within. The windows, though dusty and cracked, seemed to watch me, whispering forgotten stories.

I hesitated before pushing the gates open. The hinges groaned under the weight of time, sending a chill down my spine. As I stepped onto the overgrown pathway, flashes of my past life flickered before my eyes.

A grand party. Laughter echoing through the halls. A woman in a red dress, her eyes filled with sorrow. And then darkness.

I shook my head, trying to steady my breath. *What happened here?*

Inside, the air was thick with dust and time. The grand staircase curved like an elegant wave, its banister carved with intricate patterns—the same patterns I had once drawn. My fingers brushed against the wood, and suddenly, a name slipped from my lips before I could stop it.

"Adrian."

I froze. The name felt foreign, yet familiar. *Was that me?*

Then, a whisper echoed through the halls.

"You remember now, don't you?"

I spun around, but there was no one there. My heartbeat thundered in my ears. Had I imagined it? Or was the house speaking back to me?

Shaking off my fear, I wandered deeper inside. In the study, I found a massive oak desk covered in dust. Scattered across it were old blueprints—my blueprints. My childhood sketch had been redrawn with precise details, as if completed by an architect long before I had ever been born.

And there, in the bottom right corner, were initials: **A.L.**

I traced the letters with trembling fingers. *Adrian L...?*

Suddenly, the memory hit me like a crashing wave.

I saw myself Adrian sitting at that very desk, feverishly sketching under candlelight. My hands were stained with ink, my eyes hollow with exhaustion. There was desperation in my movements, as if I was racing against time.

A voice behind me soft, urgent.

"You must finish it before they come."

I turned, but the vision shattered. I was back in the present, gasping for breath.

Who was I finishing the city for? And who was *coming*?

Determined to find answers, I searched the study. In a locked drawer, I found a leather-bound journal. The pages were yellowed with age, but the words sent chills through my spine.

"They want to erase me. They say my designs hold power beyond architecture. If they find out the truth, they will destroy everything. But I will not let them. The city must stand."

I clutched the journal, my mind spinning. *Who were 'they'? What truth was Adrian hiding?*

A sudden creak from upstairs made my breath hitch. Someone or something was there.

I followed the sound to the attic, where an old painting was covered by a white cloth. My hands trembled as I pulled it away.

It was *him*.

Adrian L., the mysterious architect. The man who had designed this city before vanishing.

And he looked exactly like me.

I stumbled back, my chest tightening. This was no coincidence. *I was Adrian.*

Memories came flooding in of betrayal, of unfinished work, of a secret hidden within the city's design.

Then, the final piece clicked into place.

The city wasn't just architecture. It was a blueprint for something greater something that 'they' feared.

I needed to find out what it was.

Because history was repeating itself.

And this time, I would finish what I had started.

I couldn't breathe. The revelation sat heavy on my chest. I was Adrian. In another life, I had been the architect of this city one that had nearly been erased from history. But why? And by whom?

The attic felt suffocating. Dust swirled in the dim light, and the air carried a heavy, stale scent of time long forgotten. I gripped the journal tighter, scanning its last few entries for a clue.

"The city is more than stone and mortar. It is a design written in harmony with forces beyond human understanding. They fear what it will awaken."

Forces beyond understanding? What had I built?

Just then, the floor creaked again not from my own movements.

I wasn't alone.

I turned sharply, expecting to see a shadow moving in the dimness. But there was nothing—only silence, pressing against me like an unseen force.

Then, a whisper.

"You shouldn't be here."

My heart pounded. The voice was neither male nor female, not entirely human, but eerily familiar.

I grabbed the lantern from the table and backed away, my eyes darting around the room. "Who's there?" My voice came out steadier than I felt.

Silence.

Then, the attic door slammed shut behind me.

Panic surged through me. I rushed to the door, gripping the handle, but it wouldn't budge. Cold air snaked around my ankles, and suddenly, the paintings and blueprints on the walls began to flutter like they were caught in an unseen wind.

And then... I heard it.

A rhythmic *thump-thump-thump*, like footsteps echoing from another time.

I turned back toward the portrait of Adrian. But this time, his expression had changed.

His painted eyes no longer gazed forward in thought. They were looking *directly at me*.

A chill swept through my spine.

"Finish what you started."

The voice wasn't coming from the shadows. It was coming from *inside me*.

Memories surged forth, as if something had been unlocked. I saw the city *my* city just before completion. The hidden geometries, the sacred alignments, the way the buildings connected to form something greater. I hadn't just designed a city. I had designed a message.

A code.

And then... the betrayal.

The city was meant to awaken something an energy buried deep beneath its foundations. But the powerful men who funded the project had grown afraid. They called me a madman, destroyed my work, and erased my name from history.

And when I resisted?

They had me killed.

I gasped, stumbling back. The realization struck me like a lightning bolt. My death had not been an accident. It had been a warning—one meant to keep the truth buried.

And now, history was repeating itself.

Because I had returned.

And *they* knew.

SEARCH FOR THE TRUTH

The wind howled through the darkened streets as I stepped onto the pavement outside the mansion. My pulse thundered in my ears. The night was thick with shadows, the air heavy with something unseen, something that felt *alive*.

I clutched the blueprints tighter against my chest, my breath visible in the cold air. The sensation of being watched refused to fade. Every flickering streetlight, every rustling leaf it all felt like part of some unseen presence.

I forced myself to move.

The walk back to my hotel was a blur. The once-charming cobbled streets now felt like a maze closing in around me. I turned a corner too quickly, nearly colliding with a street vendor packing up for the night.

"Lo siento, señorita," he muttered, but his eyes lingered on my face for a moment too long.

I hurried on.

By the time I reached my hotel, my hands were trembling. I bolted the door behind me, my breath uneven. The room was dim, the soft glow of the bedside lamp casting long shadows over the cluttered desk. I unrolled the blueprints with shaky fingers.

And that's when I saw it.

My fingers traced the intricate lines, heart pounding. The blueprints revealed something I had overlooked before—a sigil embedded within the streets, the plazas, and the very foundation of the city. I had not just built a city.

I had built a *message*.

And that message was still waiting to be read. But before I could make sense of it, a noise shattered the silence. A soft *tap... tap... tap* at my window.

I froze.

Slowly, I turned my head.... Nothing.

The street outside was empty. The wind had died. I took a shaky breath. Probably just a loose branch or a bird

Tap... tap...

My blood ran cold.

I stood up, inching toward the window, every muscle in my body tense. My fingers gripped the curtain. I yanked it open.

No one.

Nothing.

Just the still, silent city beyond. Then, I noticed something on the glass. A symbol. Drawn in the condensation. It was the same sigil from my blueprints. I staggered back, my mind racing. Someone knew I had discovered it. And they wanted me to know *they* were watching.

I needed answers.

The next morning, I left the hotel just as the sun began to rise, the weight of the discovery pressing heavy on my chest. The library was my best chance at uncovering the truth. If this city had been built with an embedded message, then someone somewhere had to know why.

The library was an old stone building at the heart of the city, tucked between narrow alleyways. As I stepped inside, the scent of aged paper and ink wrapped around me. Dust floated in the golden morning light streaming through stained-glass windows. I approached the librarian a frail old man with silver hair and piercing blue eyes. His gaze flickered to my blueprints as I set them on the counter.

“I need information on the architect who designed this city.”

He didn’t answer right away. His fingers hovered over the pages before pulling them closer. His eyes darkened. “You shouldn’t be asking these questions,” he murmured. I leaned in. “Please. I need to know.” His gaze met mine, searching, as if deciding whether to trust me. Then, he exhaled, motioning for me to follow him into the archives.

The room smelled of damp stone, the walls lined with shelves of brittle manuscripts. The librarian pulled out a single leather-bound book, placing it on the wooden table.

The title had long faded, but as he flipped through the yellowed pages, my breath caught.

Sketches. Old, intricate city plans. And at the center

The sigil.

My sigil.

The same design embedded in the streets of the city. The same one that had appeared on my hotel window.

“This city,” the librarian murmured, “was built on something ancient. Your designs” he tapped the blueprints, “are not just architecture. They are a language. A lost knowledge buried beneath the stones.”

“A lost knowledge?” I whispered.

He nodded. “The original architect whoever he was tried to leave behind something hidden. But they erased him from history.” My throat tightened. “They erased *me*.” For the first time, I said it out loud. The librarian’s expression didn’t change. He simply nodded. “Then you already know what you must do.”

That night, I returned to the mansion. Something told me the final answer was waiting there. The doors groaned as I pushed them open, stepping inside. Moonlight spilled through the broken windows, casting eerie patterns on the dusty floor. I followed my instincts, moving through the corridors until I reached the study the place where I had found Adrian’s blueprints. I ran my fingers along the wall, searching.

Then, I felt it. A loose panel.

My heart pounded as I pried it open. Behind it, buried in the darkness, was a small, metal box. With trembling fingers, I lifted the lid. Inside was a letter. A single sheet of paper, aged and brittle. I unfolded it.

"To whoever finds this They took everything from me. But they cannot erase the truth. The city is a key. It is a door. It is not meant to be opened. Do not let them finish what I started. They are still here. Watching."

A chill ran down my spine. And then

The air shifted. A presence filled the room. I wasn't alone. The candle on the desk flickered violently, and in the reflection of the dusty mirror, I saw it

A shadow.

Not human. Not entirely *there*. I turned, my breath caught in my throat. But the room was empty. The candle went out. Darkness swallowed me whole. I ran.

Out of the mansion, into the night, the letter clutched in my fist. The city stretched before me, silent, waiting. The message was clear now. The city wasn't just a key. It was a warning. I had designed something far greater than I understood. And now, someone or something wanted it finished. Or buried. As I looked back at the mansion one last time, I knew the past had never truly left. It was still here. And it was waiting for me to remember everything. Because this story?

It wasn't over. Not yet.

I stood at the edge of history, My history. The sigil beneath my feet burned with an unseen energy, the whispers swirling in a storm around me. My past self this impossible figure of a man who should have long since faded into time watched with knowing eyes.

I didn't know how I had lived two lives, how my hands had drawn these lines before they even existed. But I knew one thing with absolute certainty:

This door was never meant to be opened. But it was *meant* to be found. My fingers hovered above the metal plate, its surface vibrating with something ancient, something waiting. I could feel the weight of the decision pressing against my ribs, my heart thundering. I had built this city, once. And I had buried something beneath it.

But *why*?

I clenched my hands into fists. There had to be a reason. I turned to the man who was me. "What's down there?" His face darkened. "Something old. Something we were never meant to touch." The shadows in the room seemed to lean forward, listening. I swallowed hard. "Then why did I make the key?" He exhaled. "Because some doors must be found, even if they are never meant to be opened." I shook my head. That wasn't enough. There was something more. Something I wasn't seeing. I pressed my palm flat against the cold surface of the plate. And the moment I did.

The world shattered.

A force surged through me, knocking the air from my lungs. I wasn't in the observatory anymore. I was somewhere *else*.

The sky above me stretched into endless gold, and beneath my feet was a city unlike any I had ever seen except I had seen it. Because I had built it. But this wasn't the city above. This was the city *beneath.* The first city. And I had been its last architect. The memories crashed into me like a flood. I saw myself the first me standing at the highest tower, drawing lines with trembling hands, whispering incantations into stone, sealing something deep beneath its bones.

This wasn't just architecture. This was a prison. And the thing beneath it, I had locked it away. Not to protect the world. But to protect *it* from the world. The realization sent a shiver through me. I had always believed I was keeping something dangerous contained. But what if it had been calling to me... because it was never the enemy? What if the real enemy had been the one who built the cage? And that enemy...

Was me.

I gasped, snapping back to reality, my knees hitting the cold floor of the observatory. The past self my reflection from another time stood motionless. I looked up at him, my breath shaky. "I wasn't protecting the world, was I?" His silence was answer enough. I had built the lock. I had buried the key in plain sight. But I had done it out of fear. And now, I had returned. To decide if the world was ready. I took a deep breath, my hand pressing once more against the door. The city around me held its breath. The shadows stilled. The whispers fell silent. This was my decision. And for the first time in lifetimes, I wasn't afraid anymore. I spoke the words I had once carved into the city's bones. *"Every line has a story."*

And then, I made my choice.

The morning sun rose over the city, its golden light stretching over rooftops, casting long shadows across the streets. The observatory doors stood open. The sigil was gone. The key had been turned. And deep beneath the city Something woke. Something that had waited for centuries. Not a monster. Not a curse. But the first architect. And for the first time in history The city would finally know the truth. The past had been rewritten. The lines had been redrawn.

THE CITY THAT AWOKE

The city stood still in the golden morning light, as if holding its breath. The streets, the archways, the towering structures I had once drawn in another life all were bathed in warmth, in the illusion of peace. I walked through the city I had created, my heart pounding, my pulse echoing in my ears. The sigil beneath the observatory was gone, the lock broken, the secret of the first architect finally released.

And yet... something still felt *wrong*.

The people around me went about their day, smiling, laughing, moving through the world like nothing had changed.

But it *had* changed. I knew it, And I wasn't the only one.

I felt it the moment I stepped into the plaza the same one I had sketched as a child, where a fountain stood at the heart of it all. The shadows of the mansion were still watching. I didn't turn my head. I didn't need to. I could feel them, clinging to the edges of the city, just beyond the reach of the morning sun.

Waiting.

That night, the city was alive with celebration. The townspeople, unaware of what had truly happened beneath their feet, filled the streets with music and laughter. Lanterns lined the cobbled pathways, flickering against the old stone. The past had been uncovered. The city's long-buried mystery had been solved. To them, this was the beginning of something new. To me, it was an ending I wasn't sure how to escape.

"You did it," a voice said beside me.

I turned to see Eva the historian who had helped me uncover the blueprints, who had stood by my side as we unraveled the truth. She held a glass of wine, her eyes filled with something unreadable. "I did *something*," I muttered. She frowned. "You don't look like someone who just solved a centuries-old mystery." Because I hadn't solved it.

I had only opened it.

"I keep thinking," I said, staring at the distant hills, "if the first architect locked something away... maybe it was for a reason." Eva hesitated, lowering her glass. "Do you regret it?" I thought about that for a long moment. Then I said, "I don't know." Because something was still watching. And it wasn't done with me yet.

Long after the celebrations ended, I stood outside the mansion. The grand, decaying structure loomed in the moonlight, its windows empty, its doors slightly ajar. The shadows had not left. If anything, they had grown darker. The city believed in its happy ending. But I knew better.

I took a slow step forward. The night air was thick with silence. Then.... A whisper, Soft. Just beyond the doorway.

He should never have opened it. My breath caught. The voice wasn't mine. And it wasn't alone.

Slowly, I stepped back, my heart hammering. The city behind me glowed with warmth, with joy, with the illusion that everything had been put to rest. But inside the mansion...Inside the bones of this place...The story was still being written.

That night, I couldn't sleep. The echoes of the past whispered in my mind, and the shadows from the mansion stayed with me, lurking in the corners of my vision even when I closed my eyes. It wasn't paranoia—it was real. Something had been released when I uncovered the city's secret. And now, it wasn't just watching.

It was waiting.

As I tossed and turned in bed, a strange sensation settled over me. It wasn't fear, exactly. It was something deeper, something I couldn't quite name.

Then, just as I drifted into uneasy sleep, I felt it a presence.

I jolted awake.

The room was cold. The air felt heavy, like something unseen had slipped in and was pressing down on my chest. I turned my head, expecting to see nothing.

But I wasn't alone.

A figure stood in the corner of the room.

Tall. Still. Familiar.

My breath caught in my throat as he stepped forward into the dim light.

It was *him*.

Adrian. My past self.

He looked exactly like the man from the old photograph the one who had designed this city lifetimes ago. His piercing eyes locked onto mine, and for the first time, I saw something in them I hadn't expected.

Fear.

"You made a mistake," he said, his voice a mere whisper.

I couldn't move. "What what do you mean?"

Adrian turned his gaze toward the window. The city stretched out before us, peaceful in the night. But his expression remained tense, haunted.

"You opened the door," he said. "But you don't understand what you let out."

I swallowed hard. "The shadows—"

"They were never supposed to return," Adrian interrupted. "That's why I locked them away."

I stared at him. "But… what *are* they?"

Adrian exhaled sharply, running a hand through his hair. "Not ghosts. Not demons. They are *memories*. Fragments of those who came before us. Architects, dreamers, builders who left their mark on this world—but whose work was never meant to be touched again."

I shuddered. "Then why are they after me?"

He turned to me, his eyes filled with something unreadable.

"Because you're the first one who ever dared to change the story."

A chill ran down my spine.

I thought back to the blueprints, to the sigil hidden in the city's design.

"I built a key," I whispered.

Adrian nodded. "And you used it. You unlocked something older than both of us."

The wind outside howled against the window. Shadows flickered against the walls, stretching unnaturally, moving even though nothing cast them.

"They're coming," Adrian said.

And then, the lights flickered.

A sharp, crackling noise filled the room, like something unseen was pressing against the walls, trying to slip through.

I turned to Adrian, panic rising in my chest. "What do we do?"

His face was grim. "We run."

We sprinted through the empty streets, the night air thick with an unnatural silence. It wasn't until we reached the city's central plaza that I finally dared to look back.

And I wished I hadn't.

The mansion stood in the distance, its windows gaping like hollow eyes. And from its doors, spilling out like ink, came the shadows.

They moved unnaturally, twisting and shifting, flickering in and out of existence. But the worst part wasn't their movement.

It was their *faces*.

Dozens of them. Eyes, mouths, twisted expressions. Not fully formed, but half-remembered.

The past was alive. And it was hunting me.

Adrian grabbed my arm. “Don’t look at them.”

We ran deeper into the city, our footsteps echoing against the stone. I could hear whispers behind us, growing louder with every step.

He should never have opened it.

He belongs to us.

Adrian led me to an old courtyard.. one I recognized instantly.

It was the place I had drawn as a child. The place where I had imagined my city’s heart would be.

He turned to me. “This is where it has to end.”

I was shaking. “How? How do we stop them?”

Adrian hesitated, and for the first time, I saw uncertainty in his eyes. “We don’t stop them. We bargain.”

A wave of cold washed over me. “Bargain with *what*?”

He pointed to the stone beneath our feet. “With the city itself.”

And that’s when I saw it—the sigil.

Not the one I had uncovered before. A different one. Hidden beneath the layers of time, waiting to be found.

It wasn’t just a key.

It was a contract.

Adrian knelt, tracing the lines with his fingers. "I made a deal once," he said. "To lock them away. To make sure they never found their way back."

I realized, then, what he was saying.

He had paid the price.

I swallowed hard. "And what do they want now?"

He looked at me. And I knew.

Me.

My vision blurred. The shadows were closing in, whispering, reaching. I felt the weight of my past pressing down on me, a lifetime I had only begun to remember.

Adrian took a deep breath. "You have a choice."

The ground beneath us pulsed. The city itself seemed to hum, waiting for my decision.

I could leave. Walk away. Pretend this had never happened.

Or...

I could finish what Adrian started.

I could make a new deal.

My heart pounded. I looked at Adrian, at the face that was somehow mine and yet not mine.

The shadows loomed closer.

And I knew.

No matter what I chose...

The city would never let me go.

The contract was still unfinished.

And the shadows were still watching.

TRAPPED ARCHITECT

The city was silent. The night stretched endlessly, but I could feel them watching, waiting. The shadows never left.

And neither could Adrian.

I stood in the heart of the plaza, staring at the sigil carved into the stone beneath my feet. The whispers had faded for now, but I knew they would return. They always did. Adrian stood beside me, his expression unreadable. He had given me a choice, but I wasn't sure if I had the strength to make it. Finally, I turned to him.

"What happens now?"

Adrian's gaze remained fixed on the ground. "Now, you learn the truth." He started walking, and without hesitation, I followed. We walked in silence through the empty streets, past towering archways and narrow alleys that twisted like a maze. The city felt different now, alive in a way I hadn't noticed before. It breathed, it remembered. Every building, every stone held memories of the past. And Adrian was one of them. He finally stopped in front of an old building, its façade worn by time. It was unlike the rest of the city, cracked walls, broken windows, forgotten.

“This was my home,” Adrian said quietly.

I hesitated before stepping inside. The air was thick with dust, the scent of old books and ink still lingering. The furniture was covered in white sheets, but beneath them, I could make out a desk covered in papers, blueprints, and unfinished sketches. It was as if time had frozen the moment Adrian disappeared. He walked forward, running his fingers along the edge of the desk. “I spent my whole life building this city. Every line, every structure, it was all meant to be perfect. I thought I was creating something beautiful.”

He turned to me, his expression dark. “But I was wrong.”

A shiver ran down my spine. “What happened?” Adrian exhaled slowly. “The shadows weren’t always here. In the beginning, they were just whispers. Doubts in my mind, voices telling me I wasn’t good enough. That I was making mistakes.” His fingers clenched into fists. “I ignored them. Kept building. I thought if I made the city perfect, the voices would stop. But the more I worked, the louder they became.”

He gestured around the room. “They started appearing in the sketches. Dark figures standing in doorways, lurking in corners. At first, I thought it was my imagination. But then..”

He hesitated, his jaw tightening.

"They stepped out of the drawings." I felt my breath hitch. "What do you mean?" Adrian looked at me, his expression unreadable. "I mean they became real." I swallowed hard. "I tried to fight them," he continued. "Destroyed the sketches, burned the blueprints. But it didn't matter. They weren't just ink on paper anymore. They were part of the city." A flickering light passed through the broken window. I turned toward the street, and for a moment, I swore I saw a shadow move between the buildings.

"They fed on my fear," Adrian said. "The more I fought them, the stronger they became." I clenched my fists. "So how did you stop them?" Adrian hesitated. "I didn't." The words sent a chill through me. "I made a deal," he said finally. "The city needed a sacrifice. And I was the only one who could pay the price."

I took a step back. "You—"

Adrian nodded. "I locked them away, but only by binding myself to the city. That's why I disappeared. That's why I can't leave." I felt a pit form in my stomach. "You're trapped." He looked at me, and for the first time, I saw the weight of his fate in his eyes. "Yes." The room fell into silence. The shadows flickered at the edges of my vision, as if listening, waiting. I turned back to the desk, staring at the faded blueprints. The city had been his masterpiece. His dream. And his prison. I clenched my jaw. "Then why did they come back?" Adrian's expression darkened.

"Because you opened the door."

I felt sick.

I had thought I was uncovering a mystery, solving a puzzle left behind by my past self. But the truth was so much worse. I had set them free. The shadows had been locked away for decades, buried beneath the weight of Adrian's sacrifice. And now, because of me, they were loose again. Adrian watched me carefully. "They won't stop now. They want more."

I swallowed hard. "More?"

He nodded. "Another sacrifice. Another architect."

The meaning behind his words hit me like a hammer.

"They want *me*."

Adrian didn't respond. He didn't have to. I took a shaky breath, my mind racing. "Then how do I stop them?" His expression remained grim. "You can't." I shook my head. "No. There has to be a way." Adrian hesitated. "There might be." I looked at him sharply. "Tell me." He exhaled slowly. "We don't fight them. We finish what I started." I frowned. "What do you mean?" Adrian turned to the blueprints, running his fingers over the lines. "I never completed the city." I blinked. "But it's already built." He shook his head. "Not all of it." He pointed to the edges of the map.

"There was supposed to be one final structure. A place that would seal the shadows forever."

I stared at the unfinished sketch. It was a building unlike any I had ever seen twisting towers, interwoven arches, lines that made no sense yet felt impossibly right. "The last piece," Adrian said softly. "The only way to lock them away for good." A part of me wanted to believe him. But something in my gut told me there was more to the story.

We spent the next few days studying the designs, searching for answers in the forgotten blueprints. The shadows still lurked, but they did not attack. They were waiting. I worked tirelessly, sketching, adjusting, trying to bring Adrian's vision to life. But the more I drew, the more something felt... wrong. It wasn't just a building. It was something more.

A doorway, A *trap*.

And I wasn't sure if it was meant for the shadows... Or for me. I turned to Adrian, my voice hesitant. "If I finish this, what happens to you?" Adrian was silent.

I felt a sinking feeling in my chest. "Adrian." He finally looked at me, and in his eyes, I saw the truth. If I completed the design, if I sealed the city's fate...

Adrian would disappear, forever.

I took a step back, my mind spinning. "No. There has to be

another way." Adrian's expression remained calm, but I could see the sadness beneath it. "This is the only way," he said. "I was never meant to stay." I clenched my fists. "That's not fair." He smiled faintly. "Neither was my life." I looked at the blueprint again, at the final piece of the city's puzzle. The lines blurred before my eyes, twisting into something I couldn't comprehend.

The shadows rustled outside, waiting. Adrian placed a hand on my shoulder. "It's your choice." My heart pounded. I had started this. I had opened the door. But now, I had to decide.

Would I finish Adrian's work and lock the shadows away forever? Or would I leave the city incomplete, knowing that the darkness would never stop hunting me? I looked up at Adrian. And then, A shadow moved behind him.

I gasped. "Adrian—"

His eyes widened.

And before I could react, The shadows struck.

Adrian's body jerked as the darkness wrapped around him.

"No!" I lunged forward, but the shadows moved faster, pulling him back into the depths of the city. His face twisted with pain, yet he didn't scream. He just looked at me, his eyes filled with a silent message.

Keep going.

Then he was gone. The room fell into darkness. The city, once alive with whispers, fell silent. And I was alone, I ran. Through the abandoned streets, past the towering structures Adrian and I had designed. The sigil beneath my feet pulsed, the very city breathing with an unnatural energy. The shadows had taken him.

But why?

I had thought they wanted me. I was supposed to be the next sacrifice. But instead, they had gone after Adrian. Unless... A chill ran down my spine. *What if Adrian had never truly escaped them?* What if, all this time, he had been living on borrowed time? My breath came in gasps as I reached the edge of the city. The blueprint was still in my hands, crumpled from my grip. The final structure—Adrian's last creation—was the key to everything. But now, I wasn't sure if I could trust it. Adrian had told me this building would seal the shadows away forever. But what if... what if that wasn't true? What if the shadows had let him believe that? What if they had *made* him design it?

I looked back toward the city, half expecting Adrian to reappear. But he didn't. The streets were empty, and the sky above was darker than it should have been. I had a choice to make. Finish the city. Or find another way.

I didn't sleep that night. I sat in my hotel room, staring at the blueprints. Every inch of my instincts told me something was wrong. The city had never been normal. It wasn't just a place, it was something alive. Something built with purpose. And now, looking at the lines, I could see it.

This wasn't just architecture. It was a *cage*. But who had been trapped inside it?

The shadows? Or Adrian?

The next morning, I went back. The streets felt different now. The air was heavy, thick with something I couldn't name. I kept my head down, moving quickly toward Adrian's old home. If there were answers, they would be there. The door creaked open under my touch. The room was untouched, as if Adrian had never left. His desk was still covered in old sketches, faded blueprints curling at the edges.

And then I saw it.

A single, torn page tucked between the stacks. The paper was yellowed with age, the ink barely legible. But as I read the words, my blood ran cold.

"I was never meant to build this city."

The words blurred before my eyes. *"They made me."* My hands trembled as I turned the page. There, beneath the frantic scrawl, was a drawing I had never seen before.

A door.

Not the final building, not the last structure Adrian had spoken of. Something else. A way *out*, I ran. Back through the city, past the silent streets, toward the place where Adrian had vanished. The shadows were waiting, lurking at the edges of my vision. But I didn't stop. I reached the sigil at the city's center, the place where everything had started. And I placed the torn page on the ground. For a moment, nothing happened. Then the ground trembled.

A deep, shuddering sound echoed through the city as the lines of the sigil shifted, rearranging themselves. The blueprints in my hands burned hot, the ink bleeding through the paper as if alive.

And then, The door appeared.

A massive stone archway rose from the ground, its surface covered in symbols I didn't recognize. A deep, endless darkness stretched beyond it.

And standing in front of it, Adrian.

He looked different. His form flickered, like a shadow caught between worlds. His eyes met mine, filled with something unreadable.

"You found it," he said. I swallowed. "What is this place?" Adrian hesitated. "The real ending." I stepped closer, my heart pounding. "What happens if I go through?" He didn't answer. Because he didn't know. The shadows moved around us, restless, hungry. They knew what was happening. They knew I had found the truth. Adrian's voice was quiet. "They won't let me leave." I clenched my fists. "Then I'll bring you with me." He smiled, but there was sadness in it.

"You can't."

The darkness behind him shifted, growing deeper. The door pulsed, as if calling to me. I turned back to the city, to the buildings Adrian and I had both built. The place where everything had started. I could stay. Finish the last structure. Complete the design. Or I could step through the door and leave it all behind. My heart pounded. Adrian's form flickered, his expression unreadable. "Go." I hesitated. The shadows moved. And then, I stepped forward. And the world disappeared.

THE RESCUE MISSION

Darkness swallowed me. I felt weightless, suspended in a void between time and space. I could still see the city behind me, fading into the distance, the echoes of its forgotten past whispering in my ears. But ahead, nothing. Just emptiness stretching forever.

And then, a voice.

"You're not supposed to be here."

It wasn't Adrian. It wasn't the shadows.

It was... Eva.

She stepped forward from the darkness, her figure barely visible against the black. But something was different. Gone was the soft-spoken woman from the town, the one who had helped me uncover the past. Now, she stood tall, her presence almost otherworldly. Her long cloak rippled in an invisible wind, her eyes glowing faintly in the darkness.

Eva had changed.

No.

Eva had always been like this. I had just never seen it before. "You knew," I whispered. "You knew about all of this." She smiled, but there was no warmth in it. "Of course I did. I was waiting for you to see it." A chill ran down my spine. "Where is Adrian?"

Her expression darkened. "Still trapped. But now we have a way to bring him back." I looked around at the nothingness surrounding us. "How?" She turned, pointing ahead. "Because you opened the door. And they made a mistake letting you in."

The shadows were shifting, moving around us, watching. I could feel them pressing in, their whispers brushing against my skin. They weren't attacking. Not yet. Eva moved quickly, pulling something from her cloak. A small silver pendant, carved with symbols that looked eerily similar to the ones on Adrian's blueprints. She pressed it into my palm.

"This will protect you," she said. "For now."

I clenched my fingers around the pendant. "For now?" Eva glanced toward the shifting darkness ahead. "They know you're here. They won't let Adrian go so easily. But we have a chance if we move fast." She stepped forward, and I followed. The shadows parted for her.

The deeper we went, the more the world changed. The void was no longer empty. Shapes began to emerge, half-formed structures, broken bridges, towers that seemed to melt into the sky. It was like walking through an unfinished dream, a city that had been erased but never truly forgotten.

And at its center, a massive structure stood—twisted and unnatural, like something that had been built and then rewritten over and over again. "That's where they're keeping him," Eva said.

A tower.

But not just any tower. It was the final structure Adrian had designed. The one he had believed would seal the shadows away. But instead, it had become their throne. The air grew heavier as we approached. The whispers turned into a low hum, a sound that vibrated through my bones.

"They know," I said.

Eva nodded. "They've always known."

We reached the base of the tower. A massive iron door loomed before us, covered in shifting symbols. The same sigils Adrian had once drawn, now pulsing with dark energy.

Eva placed her hand on the door. "This will be the hard part." The moment she spoke, the shadows moved. They rose from the ground, from the walls, from the very air itself. No longer just wisps of darkness but towering figures with hollow eyes and jagged limbs. They surrounded us, forming a wall of living night.

Eva didn't flinch. She raised her other hand, revealing a second pendant, identical to the one she had given me. And then she shattered it against the door. A pulse of blinding white light erupted outward. The shadows screamed, recoiling from the energy. The door trembled, the symbols flashing wildly.

And then it opened.

Inside, the air was suffocating. The walls pulsed, alive with some unseen force. The hallways twisted and shifted, leading in circles, designed to keep us lost forever.

Eva moved fast, navigating the labyrinth as if she had seen it before. "How do you know the way?" I asked. She didn't answer. Finally, we reached the top of the tower.

Adrian was there.

Suspended in the air, his body surrounded by the same dark tendrils that had taken him. His eyes were closed, his face pale.

He looked... empty.

Eva stepped forward. "It's time to bring him back." I moved toward him, but the shadows struck first. The tower shook as they surged forward, their forms solidifying into monstrous shapes. Eva pulled out another pendant, but before she could use it, a massive force threw her back against the wall.

I barely had time to react before the shadows turned on me. Then, Adrian's voice rang out.

"Stop."

The shadows froze. Adrian's eyes opened. For a moment, everything was silent. Then he broke free.

The explosion of light was blinding. The tendrils shattered, the darkness recoiling as Adrian collapsed to the floor. I rushed forward, grabbing his arm before he could fall.

His breathing was ragged, his body weak. But he was alive. Eva staggered to her feet, her eyes narrowing at the swirling shadows. "They won't stop," she said. "Not until they take something in return." Adrian's grip tightened on my wrist.

"They can't have me," he said.

Eva's expression was unreadable. "Then they'll take someone else." The realization hit me like a punch to the gut. The shadows needed someone. They had kept Adrian because he had designed the city, because his lines had built their world.

If he left, Someone had to take his place.

The shadows attacked. Eva moved first, dragging me and Adrian toward the open doorway. The entire tower shook, the walls collapsing around us.

We ran.

Through the twisting corridors, down the endless staircase, past the creatures clawing at our heels. The exit was just ahead. We burst through the doors, the shadows screaming behind us. The moment Adrian stepped outside, the world shifted. The city trembled. The structures changed.

And then, Silence.

The shadows were gone. For now.

Adrian swayed beside me, exhausted. Eva stood a few feet away, watching the city with an expression I couldn't read. The world around us was different. The city was no longer suffocating. The air felt lighter. But something was wrong.

I turned to Adrian. "Are you okay?"

He nodded, but there was hesitation in his eyes. Eva exhaled, stepping forward. "We did it," I said. "You're free." She gave me a look that made my stomach drop.

"For now," she said.

That's when I felt it. A low hum in the air. A whisper in the wind. And then, Laughter. Not Adrian's. Not Eva's.

But the shadows.

The laughter never stopped.

It echoed through the streets, slipping through cracks in the buildings, seeping into the air like a sickness. It was deep, hollow, layered, like a thousand voices speaking at once. The city was no longer silent. It was alive with something dark. Adrian and I stood frozen in the middle of the empty street, the laughter pressing against us, curling around our skin like invisible tendrils.

And then the screams started.

Far off at first, rising from the distant alleys, then closer, coming from the homes that should have been empty. The whole town had been asleep, locked away in their quiet lives, pretending nothing had ever happened here. But now, the shadows had returned.

And they were hungry.

Eva grabbed my arm, her grip cold. "We need to go. Now." I didn't move. Not yet. My eyes were locked on the darkness creeping along the walls, stretching toward the light like it had learned something new.

Adrian swayed beside me, barely standing. He was free, but not whole. The shadows had drained something from him, and I wasn't sure if he would ever get it back.

And then there was Eva.

I turned to her. She was focused, sharp, moving with certainty like she had always known this was coming. Like she had planned for it. I had trusted her before. But now? I wasn't sure who or what she really was.

She pulled us into the narrow backstreets, moving fast. The town was a maze of forgotten roads, abandoned places that had never quite fit into the world. The deeper we went, the more the city seemed to twist, bending in ways that defied logic.

Adrian stumbled, and I caught him, his breath ragged. His body was too cold. Eva glanced back. "We can't stop here." I tightened my grip on Adrian's arm. "We need answers first. What's happening?" She hesitated. Just for a second. But it was enough.

"Something's wrong," she admitted. "This wasn't supposed to happen." Her voice was steady, but there was an edge to it. A hesitation she hadn't shown before. I narrowed my eyes. "And how would you know that?"

Eva didn't answer.

The streets were empty, but we weren't alone. The laughter had stopped. But now, the whispers had begun. Soft voices curling through the air, speaking words that didn't belong to this world. I couldn't understand them, but Adrian his face changed. His hands trembled. His breath hitched.

He knew what they were saying.

Eva pulled him forward, her movements urgent. "They're calling for him. We need to move." "Where?" I demanded. "Where are we going?" She turned a corner sharply, leading us toward a building I didn't recognize. It was old, forgotten, tucked between taller structures like it had been placed there as an afterthought. She shoved open the door.

"Inside. Now."

The room was dark, lit only by the weak moonlight filtering through broken windows. The air smelled of dust and something old, like a memory that had never faded. Adrian collapsed onto a worn-out couch, his body shaking. I stepped forward, my voice sharp. "Who are you, Eva?"

She didn't react right away. She stood by the window, watching the streets, her fingers twitching like she was waiting for something.

Finally, she turned.

"You really don't remember me?" Her words hit me like a blow.

I froze.

"What are you talking about?" Adrian stirred. His voice was weak but clear. "Eva... who are you?" For the first time, she looked uncertain. She glanced at Adrian, then at me, then back out the window. "The shadows," she said finally, "they don't just take people. They take memories."

The room felt colder.

"You knew me," she continued. "Before all of this. Before the city. Before Adrian built the key. We fought the shadows once before." I shook my head. "I would remember that."

She gave a sad smile. "Would you?"

I opened my mouth, but no words came.

Because somewhere, deep in the back of my mind, something shifted.

A forgotten piece of a memory. A voice, calling my name.

Eva's voice.

Adrian groaned, pressing a hand to his head. The whispers outside were growing louder.

"They're getting stronger," Eva said. "We don't have much time."

She knelt beside Adrian, pulling something from her pocket, a small vial filled with a dark, swirling liquid.

He flinched. "What is that?"

"Something to keep them out of your head."

He hesitated. "And if I don't take it?"

"They'll come for you," she said. "And this time, they won't let go."

Adrian swallowed hard. Then, slowly, he reached for the vial.

As he drank, the room shook.

A deep, guttural growl echoed through the streets outside.

Eva's face darkened.

"They know we're here."

The shadows moved.

Not like before. This wasn't creeping darkness, slithering through cracks.

This was a storm.

A flood of writhing figures pouring through the streets, bending the very air around them. Their hunger was endless. Their power was stronger.

Adrian gasped, his body seizing up.

Eva grabbed my wrist. "We have to run."

"But—"

She didn’t let me argue. She pulled me toward the back door, and I barely had time to drag Adrian with me.

The moment we stepped outside, the sky itself changed.

The moonlight dimmed, swallowed by something unseen. The buildings trembled.

And then, the laughter returned.

Louder. Closer.

And this time, it spoke.

"You think you won?"

The words weren’t whispered. They were inside me. Crawling through my thoughts, wrapping around my mind like vines.

Eva stiffened.

"They’re learning," she murmured.

I turned to her. "What does that mean?"

She met my eyes.

"It means," she said quietly, "they’re not just shadows anymore."

We ran.

Through the twisting alleys, past the empty streets, moving faster than our bodies should have allowed.

But the shadows followed.

And they were laughing.

Adrian's breathing was shallow, his body weak. He wasn't free. Not completely.

And Eva—

I still didn't know if I could trust her.

But for now, she was the only one keeping us alive.

The city stretched ahead, the darkness closing in behind us.

And somewhere, deep in the heart of it all, the shadows were waiting.

Watching.

Hungry.

And we had only just begun to run.

The night stretched on, endless and suffocating. The streets of the abandoned town twisted in ways that didn't make sense, folding into themselves like a maze designed to keep us trapped.

And the shadows knew it.

Their laughter had faded, but their presence remained—watching, waiting. I could feel them slithering behind us, just beyond the edges of sight.

Eva led the way, her steps steady despite the chaos around us. She wasn't afraid. Or if she was, she hid it well.

Adrian, finally able to stand on his own, moved beside me. His face was pale, his body still weak from the rescue, but his mind was sharper now.

"We need a way out," he muttered. "Before they come back."

Eva glanced at him but didn't slow down.

"I'm working on it."

We moved through the town like ghosts. The buildings around us were broken things, their windows shattered, their doors hanging loose on rusted hinges. It looked like a place forgotten by time, a place that had never really been part of the world.

Adrian tugged at my sleeve, his voice low. "We need to talk."

I nodded, slowing my pace as Eva continued ahead.

"What is it?"

He hesitated. Then, "Something's wrong with her."

I frowned. "Eva?"

He nodded. "She knows too much. She moves through this town like she's been here before. And the shadows—" He swallowed. "They're afraid of her."

I hadn't noticed it at first. But now, looking at the way she walked, the way she kept checking the buildings, the way her fingers twitched like she was waiting for something to happen...

Adrian was right.

Eva wasn't just a survivor.

She was something else entirely.

The shadows didn't attack again. Not yet. But they were near.

I could feel them shifting in the air, curling around the edges of the buildings, stretching along the ground in thin tendrils of darkness.

And Eva—

She wasn't just leading us. She was guiding us.

Like she knew exactly where to go.

Adrian clenched his fists. "I don't trust her."

I didn't answer.

Because I wasn't sure if I trusted her either.

But I knew one thing.

We didn’t have another choice.

Finally, Eva stopped.

We stood before a wall—an old, crumbling structure covered in strange markings. It didn’t belong here. It looked... ancient.

She pressed a hand against it.

For a moment, nothing happened. Then—

The air shifted.

A faint glow pulsed beneath her fingertips, spreading outward in slow, deliberate waves. The markings on the wall responded, lighting up with a soft, eerie light.

Adrian stiffened. "What the hell—"

Eva didn’t explain. She just pushed.

And the wall opened.

A deep, hollow space stretched before us—a tunnel, descending into the earth.

Eva turned to face us. "Inside. Now."

Adrian took a step back. "No. No way. What is this?"

Eva sighed. "A way out."

I hesitated. "Where does it lead?"

She met my gaze.

"Somewhere the shadows can’t reach."

I didn’t know if that was true. But I did know one thing.

The shadows wanted us to stay up here.

Which meant we had to go down.

The tunnel smelled of damp stone and something old, something buried beneath time itself.

Eva moved ahead, guiding us through the darkness. The deeper we went, the more the air changed. It felt heavier, charged with something I didn’t understand.

Adrian walked beside me, his shoulders tense. He wasn’t shaking anymore. He was recovering. But his mind was still troubled.

"You’re feeling it too, right?" he murmured.

I nodded.

There was power here. Not the kind the shadows carried. Something older.

Something that felt almost... alive.

And Eva—

She wasn't struggling at all.

She moved through the tunnel like she had walked this path a thousand times before.

Like she belonged here.

Finally, the tunnel opened into a vast underground chamber.

I stopped breathing.

The place was massive stone walls stretching high above us, covered in symbols that glowed with a soft, silver light. Strange structures stood in the distance, worn with age but still intact.

It wasn't just a tunnel.

It was a city.

Adrian took a shaky step forward. "What... is this place?"

Eva didn't answer right away. She looked around, her expression unreadable. Then, finally—

"It was a home once."

Adrian tensed. "Yours?"

She exhaled. "A long time ago."

I stared at her, something clicking into place. "You're from here."

She hesitated.

Then—

"Yes."

Adrian shook his head. "No. That's not possible. This place—it's been buried for centuries."

Eva turned to face him. "And yet, here I am."

He looked at me, frustration in his eyes. "Tell me you don't believe this."

But I did.

Because it made sense now.

The way Eva moved. The way she knew the shadows. The way she fought them.

She wasn't just some town helper.

She was something else.

Something older.

And the shadows—

They feared her.

The ground trembled.

Eva’s expression darkened. "They found us."

Adrian turned toward the tunnel entrance, his face pale.

The shadows were here.

Moving fast, pouring through the passage like a living tide.

Eva took a slow breath.

And then—

She raised her hands.

The air crackled.

A pulse of energy rippled through the chamber, slamming into the shadows like a wave. They screeched, recoiling from her power, twisting in pain.

Adrian stared, stunned.

I could barely breathe.

Eva wasn’t just fighting them.

She was breaking them.

The shadows shrieked, pulling back, retreating into the darkness.

For the first time, they were afraid.

Eva lowered her hands, her breathing steady. The glow in her eyes faded, but the power was still there, thrumming beneath her skin.

Adrian took a step toward her. "What... are you?"

Eva met his gaze, something unreadable in her expression.

"You're not ready for that answer."

Adrian clenched his fists. "I deserve to know."

Eva tilted her head. "Do you?"

I placed a hand on Adrian's shoulder. "She just saved us."

He exhaled, tension still in his body. But he didn't argue.

Because one thing was clear.

Eva was not just another survivor.

She was something else entirely.

And the shadows?

They weren't gone.

Not yet.

But for now, they were watching.

Waiting.

And the next time they came...

They wouldn't hold back.

THE FORGOTTEN CITY

The tunnel walls widened, and suddenly, we stepped into light.

For a moment, none of us spoke.

The underground city stretched before us, vast and untouched by time. Golden towers rose into the cavern's high ceiling, their tips glowing with an unnatural luminescence. The streets, paved with something smooth and reflective like obsidian, pulsed with veins of silver light, tracing intricate patterns beneath our feet. Waterfalls cascaded from unseen sources, their streams flowing through sculpted channels that wound through the city like glowing rivers.

Adrian sucked in a sharp breath. "This was buried beneath the town?"

Eva stood ahead of us, her posture unreadable. "Yes."

I turned in slow circles, taking it all in. The beauty of the place was overwhelming. Unlike the abandoned ruins above, this city was alive. The air itself seemed to hum with energy, carrying the scent of something floral, something ancient.

Adrian turned to Eva. "What is this place?"

She hesitated, then finally said, "This is where I was born."

We walked forward, deeper into the city. The roads were lined with empty houses, their doors slightly ajar as if waiting for someone to return.

"This doesn't make sense," I murmured. "If this place is so powerful, why did it disappear? Why is no one here?"

Eva exhaled. "Because they're gone."

"Gone where?" Adrian pressed.

Eva didn't look at him. "Dead."

A chill ran through me.

Adrian frowned. "All of them?"

She nodded.

I glanced at the city again, suddenly seeing it differently. The beauty remained, but now it felt... hollow. A place built to thrive, left to decay.

Adrian clenched his fists. "What happened?"

Eva finally turned to us. Her face was calm, but there was something heavy in her gaze.

"It's time I told you the truth."

She led us to what looked like an ancient temple at the city's center. Inside, the walls were covered in carvings stories etched into stone.

Eva ran her fingers along the carvings. "This city was once a sanctuary. A place of knowledge, power... and protection."

I looked at the carvings. They showed figures with glowing eyes, surrounded by swirling energy, standing against something dark.

"The shadows?" I whispered.

Eva nodded. "They weren't always this strong. We kept them at bay for centuries. This city... it was built as a shield against them."

Adrian narrowed his eyes. "Then what changed?"

Eva's fingers stilled.

"They learned."

She walked toward a raised platform in the center of the temple and knelt beside it. "My people were gifted. We could manipulate energy light, power, even time." She looked up at us. "We weren't human. Not entirely."

Adrian took a step back. "What are you saying?"

Eva met his gaze.

"My people weren't from this world."

The words hung in the air.

I struggled to process them. "Then... where?"

She exhaled. "We were travelers, explorers. We arrived here long ago, seeking refuge from something worse than the shadows. We built this city to protect ourselves... and in doing so, we became part of this world."

Adrian's jaw tightened. "And the shadows?"

"They were already here," Eva admitted. "Lurking in the dark places, waiting for something strong enough to challenge them."

I swallowed. "And that was you?"

Eva nodded.

Adrian's voice was sharp. "If you were strong enough to fight them, why did your people die?"

Eva's expression darkened. "Because the shadows tricked us. They couldn't defeat us in battle, so they learned to corrupt. They whispered in the minds of our strongest warriors, turning them against us.

"Our defenses fell from within."

I shivered.

Adrian looked around. "So what happened to the last of you?"

Eva closed her eyes. "I was the only one left."

Silence filled the temple.

Eva finally continued, "Before the city fell, we locked it away. Sealed it beneath the earth to keep its power out of the shadows' reach." She looked at me. "That's why I stayed in the town above. To make sure no one ever found it."

Adrian's expression was unreadable. "Then why bring us here now?"

Eva's gaze darkened.

"Because the shadows are stronger than before. And if they find this place..."

She didn't finish the sentence.

She didn't need to.

We all understood.

Adrian sat on the temple steps, running a hand through his hair. "So let me get this straight. You're an alien. Your people built a secret underground city to fight shadows.

And now that we've found it, the shadows are about to unleash hell trying to claim it?"

Eva nodded.

He let out a hollow laugh. "Great. Just great."

I took a deep breath. "Then we need to figure out how to stop them."

Eva met my gaze. "That's why I brought you here."

Adrian frowned. "Us?"

"You," she corrected. "Both of you."

I stared at her. "Why?"

Eva's lips pressed into a thin line.

"Because you were never supposed to find this place."

Adrian stiffened. "What does that mean?"

Eva hesitated. Then, finally—

"It means the city called you here."

A shiver ran through me. "What are you saying?"

She stepped forward, touching my arm lightly. "You both felt it, didn't you? The pull. The feeling that you had to keep digging, keep searching. That wasn't an accident. The city wanted you to come."

Adrian shook his head. "Why us?"

Eva's gaze softened. "Because you are meant to finish what my people started."

Before we could respond, a distant sound echoed through the chamber.

Laughter.

Cold. Hollow. Familiar.

The shadows.

Adrian's breath hitched. "They're already here."

Eva turned toward the temple doors, her hands glowing faintly. "They were always coming."

The light in the city flickered.

I could feel it something shifting, something awakening.

Eva's voice was quiet, but firm.

"This fight isn't over yet."

The shadows weren't coming.

Not yet.

For the first time in what felt like ages, there was silence. No whispers slithering through the dark, no cold presence crawling along my skin. But that silence wasn't comforting. It felt like a pause before the storm.

Adrian, Eva, and I stood in the center of the hidden city, its golden glow dimmed as if the very walls were holding their breath. We had time. Not much, but enough to search for answers.

And we needed answers.

We walked through the abandoned streets, following the faint pulsing lights embedded in the roads. The city was vast, and though it felt empty, it wasn't dead. It was waiting. Adrian's eyes scanned the towering structures, his fingers twitching at his side. "I need to see the blueprints again."

I unzipped my bag and pulled out the crumpled papers—the ones I had stolen from the attic before everything fell apart. Adrian took them, spreading them on a smooth stone table in what might have once been a gathering hall. His expression darkened.

"They forced me to make these," he muttered. "They wouldn't let me stop. And now I know why."

Eva and I leaned over, studying the lines and measurements.

"These are just the plans for the town above," I said. "The buildings, the streets—"

Adrian jabbed a finger at a particular pattern woven into the layout. "No. Look closer."

I did.

And then I saw it.

The design of the town above wasn't random. It mirrored something—a symbol, a sigil built into the ground itself. And that sigil wasn't just decoration.

It was a seal.

A lock.

A barrier.

The town above had been constructed to keep something in.

And now, with the door open, that lock had been broken.

Adrian let out a sharp breath. "They used me. They needed me to redraw this town over and over. Every time the lock weakened, they forced me to reinforce it. But something changed. The barrier started failing faster than they could repair it."

Eva's expression darkened. "Because the city's power is fading."

My heart pounded. "So the shadows weren't just keeping you prisoner. They were using you to keep themselves trapped."

Adrian nodded. "Until they found another way out."

I exhaled. "Me."

I was the one who had opened the door.

Eva turned away, her arms crossed. "It was never about you," she said quietly. "It was about the key."

Adrian's gaze snapped to her. "The key..."

Eva didn't respond. She walked to one of the walls, placing her palm flat against it. The stone rippled beneath her touch, revealing glowing symbols.

Then, with a slow breath, she finally spoke.

"I wasn't just living in the town above to keep watch," she admitted. "I was waiting. Waiting for the one who would bring back the key."

I took a shaky step forward. "What key? I never—"

Eva turned, her gaze locked on mine.

"The one you used to open the door," she said.

I blinked. "But that was just a—" I reached into my bag, my fingers closing around the cool metal of the old, rusted key I had found in the attic.

Or at least, I had thought it was just an old key.

Now, as I pulled it out into the light, I saw it for what it really was.

It wasn't rusted.

It was covered in engraved symbols, ancient carvings that glowed faintly at my touch.

This wasn't an ordinary key.

It was a piece of the city itself.

A key meant to unlock something long buried.

And I had given the shadows exactly what they needed.

Adrian clenched his fists. "So the shadows waited all this time just to get their hands on this?"

Eva's expression was grim. "Not just the key. The city's power is fading, but it isn't gone yet. They still need one last thing to take control of it completely."

I swallowed. "What?"

Eva hesitated. Then, slowly, she pointed to Adrian.

"Him."

Silence.

Adrian stiffened. "What do you mean, me?"

Eva's voice was quiet but steady. "You were never just a prisoner. They didn't just keep you locked away to draw blueprints. They bound you to this city. You and the shadows are connected now."

Adrian shook his head. "No. I never—I never asked for that—"

"They didn't ask. They took it from you," Eva said. "Every year, every decade they kept you, they weren't just holding you prisoner. They were turning you into part of the seal itself."

My stomach twisted. "That's why they wouldn't let him die."

Eva nodded.

Adrian's hands trembled. "So what? If they kill me now, they win?"

Eva's lips pressed into a thin line. "No. If they kill you, they lose their last link to the city's power. That's why they can't let you die."

Adrian let out a hollow laugh. "That's comforting."

I gripped the key tighter. "Then we have to destroy them before they take that last piece."

Eva glanced down at the key in my hand. "We have to destroy this before they use it to finish what they started."

We spent hours searching through the temple's archives, piecing together the city's forgotten history.

And that's when we found it.

The way to destroy the shadows.

Or rather... the only way.

My breath caught in my throat as I read the ancient text. "This... this can't be right."

Adrian leaned over my shoulder, his face pale. "Eva. Tell me this is some kind of mistake."

She didn't answer.

Because we all knew it was the truth.

The only way to end the shadows was to end the city itself.

And everything inside it.

The golden towers. The glowing rivers. The last remnants of Eva's people.

Everything.

Eva closed her eyes, her hands trembling at her sides.

"I knew this would be the answer," she whispered. "I just didn't want to believe it."

Adrian ran a hand through his hair, his expression twisted with frustration. "There has to be another way."

"There isn't," Eva said, her voice barely above a whisper. "The city is the only thing keeping them bound. If we destroy it, we destroy them."

I swallowed hard. "But that means—"

Eva nodded. "Once we do this, there's no going back."

The shadows would never let us destroy their prison.

They would fight with everything they had.

And even if we succeeded… we had no idea what would happen next.

The city might crumble.

The town above might collapse.

Eva might disappear forever.

And Adrian…

Adrian's fate was the most uncertain of all.

He looked down at the blueprints, at the key still glowing faintly in my hands.

Then, slowly, he exhaled.

"If this is the only way," he said, his voice steady, "then we have no choice."

Eva met his gaze. "Are you sure?"

Adrian let out a dry chuckle. "Not even a little bit."

I took a deep breath.

We had found the answer.

Now, we just had to survive long enough to use it.

FOUNDATION

The city breathed.

Not in the way living things did, but in the way structures held onto memories. Every pillar, every bridge, every archway in this hidden place told a story. And if I listened carefully, I could almost hear the whispers woven into the stone.

Adrian, Eva, and I stood in the heart of it, staring at the glowing blueprint sprawled across the floor of an ancient hall. The answer was here. Somewhere in these walls, these roads, these very foundations.

And the dead were watching.

For centuries, architects believed that every line drawn had a purpose. Every wall separated spaces, every corridor led somewhere, and every door even the locked ones had a reason to exist.

But this city had doors that were never meant to be opened.

And I had forced one open.

Adrian had been used to redraw this place over and over, but now we saw the deeper truth the city wasn't just a structure.

It was a body.

The streets were veins. The buildings were bones. The towers, ribs protecting its heart.

But the shadows... they were its sickness. And like any disease, they were trying to spread.

If we destroyed the city, we might stop them.

But what if the city was never meant to be destroyed?

Eva traced her fingers along the ancient carvings on the wall. "You said something before... about every line having a purpose. What if this city was never just a prison?"

I frowned. "What do you mean?"

Eva turned to Adrian. "Think. When you were trapped, when they forced you to rebuild this place what did they make you change?"

Adrian hesitated. "They always focused on the center. The main plaza, the heart of the city. Every time the structure weakened, they forced me to reinforce it."

My breath caught. "So they weren't just trying to keep themselves in."

Eva nodded. "They were trying to keep something else out."

I looked back at the blueprint.

The sigil in the center of the city it wasn't just a seal.

It was a barrier.

But if the shadows were so desperate to maintain it, then... what exactly were they afraid of?

My fingers traced the outer edges of the map, following the delicate patterns carved into the stone floor. And that's when I saw it.

An extra layer.

Hidden beneath the surface of the city.

A second foundation, buried deep underground, holding something beneath it.

Adrian's eyes darkened. "This city... it's built on top of something, isn't it?"

Eva swallowed. "Yes."

I turned to her. "You knew?"

She hesitated. "Not everything. But I knew enough to understand that this city was hiding more than it revealed."

Adrian's jaw clenched. "And now we've disturbed it."

The ground trembled beneath our feet.

Not from an earthquake. Not from shadows creeping closer.

But from something below.

Something waking up.

Eva's expression was unreadable. "We have to go deeper."

"Deeper?" Adrian echoed. "Into what?"

Eva exhaled. "The real city."

I blinked. "You mean—"

Eva nodded. "This place? What we see now? This is just the surface. The city that once was—the original city—was buried long ago."

I stared down at the glowing blueprint. "And you think the answers are down there?"

Eva met my gaze.

"I know they are."

The three of us moved quickly, following the intricate pathways etched into the walls. The city had secrets, and we were about to uncover the deepest one.

But as we descended into the tunnels below, I felt it again—

We were being watched.

But not by the shadows.

No, this was something else.

Something older.

The air grew colder as we walked, the walls shifting from gold to dark stone. The deeper we went, the less the city looked alive.

This place had been abandoned.

Or so we thought.

At the bottom of the tunnel, we found the first body.

It lay against the wall, wrapped in tattered robes. A builder, an architect.

A man who had drawn lines and told stories through stone just like Adrian.

His hands still clutched a broken chisel.

And beneath him, carved into the wall with his final strength, were words in an ancient language.

Eva knelt, tracing the letters. She whispered the translation under her breath:

"They were never the prisoners. We were."

My blood turned to ice.

Adrian took a step back. "No. No, that can't be right."

I turned, shining the lantern farther into the darkness.

There were more.

Bodies lined the tunnels. Architects. Builders. An entire city's worth of people.

Not just dead.

Buried alive.

Eva's voice trembled. "This city wasn't built to hold the shadows."

I swallowed hard. "Then what was it built for?"

She exhaled.

"To keep us inside."

And that's when the shadows laughed.

The shadows laughed. A slow, eerie sound that echoed through the underground chambers, bouncing off the ancient stone walls. It wasn't the laughter of something amused it was something that knew we had finally seen the truth.

The city had never been built to contain the shadows. It had been built to contain us.

And those who came before us had already paid the price.

Adrian’s fingers trembled as he reached out to touch the carved words left behind by the dead architect. "They were never the prisoners. We were."

His breath came in shallow gasps. "Then why did they keep me alive? Why force me to build the city over and over again?"

Eva's expression darkened. "Because they needed you to repair the cage. They needed you to keep reinforcing their prison while they fed on the city above."

My stomach twisted. "And when they were strong enough..."

Eva finished my sentence. "They started expanding it. Taking more people. Feeding off them."

Adrian's voice was hollow. "Like they did to these architects."

We stood in silence, the weight of the realization pressing down on us like the very stones of the city. The shadows had won before. They had taken this place once. And they would do it again.

But then, the air shifted.

And the dead began to move.

It started with the faintest flicker of light. A golden shimmer rippling through the dust-filled air. Then, one by one, the figures around us straightened not alive, but not entirely dead either.

Their hollow eyes glowed, their skeletal hands raised toward the walls, tracing symbols in the air. Blueprints.

I watched, heart pounding, as the glowing lines formed into patterns. Buildings, streets, towers but not the city above.

It was a different city. The original city.

And in the very center, a structure unlike anything I had seen before.

A weapon.

Eva stepped forward cautiously, her voice barely above a whisper. "They're showing us something."

Adrian's eyes widened as the ancient architects' movements grew more frantic. Their translucent fingers sketched faster, their golden blueprints pulsing with energy.

Then, they stopped.

The air crackled.

And the light exploded outward, forming a single word in the center of the blueprint.

KEYSTONE.

I turned to Eva. "Keystone? Like an actual stone?"

Adrian frowned. "No... keystones are the central piece of an arch. The thing that holds everything together."

Eva inhaled sharply. "Then it means..."

I finished the thought. "The city has a weak point."

Adrian's gaze darkened. "And if we destroy it—"

Eva swallowed. "We bring the whole thing down."

The dead had given us the answer. But could we really do it?

Could we destroy the entire city to kill the shadows?

The golden figures flickered, their light dimming. They had given us all they could. One by one, they turned, their hollow eyes watching us with something that almost looked like... relief.

Then, as quickly as they had appeared, they were gone.

Silence.

For the first time since stepping into this underground world, the city felt empty.

I exhaled. "We have a way to stop them."

Adrian nodded, his expression grim. "But they'll never let us get to it."

Eva's jaw tightened. "Then we make sure they don't stop us."

Above us, the shadows stirred.

And the hunt began.

The shadows were screaming. A piercing, inhuman wail that shattered the air, vibrating through the very stones beneath our feet.

The keystone was breaking.

I could feel it. The ancient structure that held this entire underground world together was crumbling, its power unraveling like threads of an old tapestry. The city that had been hidden for centuries the one the shadows had fought to control was finally coming undone.

But so was everything else.

Adrian stood at the heart of the collapsing chamber, his hands pressed against the keystone, his face pale but determined. The golden symbols left by the dead architects pulsed around him, their last gift guiding him through the destruction.

"We don't have time!" I shouted, grabbing his arm. "We have to get out of here!"

But he didn't move.

His gaze locked onto mine, something unspoken in his expression.

Eva's voice broke through the chaos, her eyes wild. "It has to be someone from the past," she whispered. "Someone who was bound to this city... to the shadows."

I froze. "No."

Adrian smiled. A tired, broken smile.

"This was always the way it had to end."

Before I could stop him, he turned back to the keystone, pressing both palms against the ancient stone. The symbols ignited, burning into his skin, etching his very soul into the collapsing foundation.

The shadows shrieked louder, realizing what was happening.

They lunged for him, desperate, clawing, writhing but it was too late.

The keystone cracked.

A blinding white light exploded from its center, tearing through the chamber, through the city, through the shadows themselves.

And then—

Silence.

The ground beneath us trembled. The walls began to dissolve into dust. The golden blueprints that had once mapped this forgotten world flickered out, one by one.

The underground city—the place that had held so many secrets—was fading.

And so was Eva.

She stood a few feet away, her expression unreadable as her form flickered like a dying flame.

I stepped toward her. "Eva?"

She smiled softly, but there was sadness in her eyes. "This city was my home. My prison. My purpose."

"No," I whispered, shaking my head. "No, you can leave with me. We can go back—"

She lifted a hand, and for the first time, I saw the truth.

She had never been part of my world.

Eva belonged to the city. To its magic. To the past.

And now that the city was gone... so was she.

Her body flickered again, her edges blurring like mist.

She took one last step toward me and pressed something into my hand.

The key. The same one I had used to open the door. The same one that had brought me here.

Her fingers curled over mine. "You were always meant to find this place."

I shook my head, my throat tight. "But I don’t understand"

"You will," she whispered.

And then she was gone.

The world around me shattered.

The underground city collapsed, swallowing itself whole. The streets, the buildings, the remnants of the past all of it disintegrated, vanishing into the void.

The last thing I heard was the wind.

And then—

Darkness.

I gasped.

Cold air rushed into my lungs. My eyes flew open.

I was lying on the cobblestone streets of the town above the town I had drawn as a child.

The underground world was gone. No traces remained. No shadows. No magic.

No Adrian.

No Eva.

Just me.

And the key.

I curled my fingers around the metal, my heart pounding. I didn't know how much time had passed, how I had gotten here, or if any of it had even been real.

But as I stood, looking around the town the one I had once sketched without ever knowing why I realized something.

Every line an architect draws has a story.

And some stories never truly end.

ABOUT THE AUTHOR

I am an architect who believes that buildings are not only made of bricks and plans they are made of feelings, stories, and the quiet spaces in between.

Long before I ever held a pencil to draw a wall, I was a wanderer. I grew up fascinated by hidden corners: old staircases, locked rooms, and overgrown courtyards where time seemed to stand still.

Over the years, my work has taken me to modern cities and shiny new projects. But again and again, I found myself drawn to places most people overlook the abandoned, the half-ruined, the nearly forgotten.

It was in these places that I felt something unexplainable, something true: the echo of lives that came before and the possibility of finding pieces of ourselves in spaces no one else notices anymore.

When I am not sketching or writing, you can find me exploring old neighborhoods with my camera, sitting beside a quiet river, or simply wondering about all the unseen worlds behind closed doors.

This book is my invitation to you to slow down, look closer, and remember that beauty and meaning often live in the places we think are empty.

If you ever find yourself in Rishikesh, or anywhere that feels ancient and alive, I hope you, too, will listen for the whispers of forgotten stories and maybe discover something about your own.

www.ingramcontent.com/pod-product-compliance
Lightning Source LLC
Chambersburg PA
CBHW062111160726
48282CB00026B/750
* 9 7 8 9 3 3 4 0 6 5 0 9 1 *